Rock

Written by *Jillian Powell*

Illustrated by *Anthony Williams*

FULL FLIGHT

Titles in Full Flight Girl Power

Badger Publishing Limited
Oldmedow Road,
Hardwick Industrial Estate,
King's Lynn PE30 4JJ
Telephone: 01438 791037
www.badgerlearning.co.uk

2 4 6 8 10 9 7 5 3

Rock Chick ISBN 978 1 84691 026 5

Series Editor: Jonny Zucker
Publisher: David Jamieson
Commissioning Editor: Carrie Lewis
Editor: Paul Martin
Design: Fiona Grant
Illustration: Anthony Williams

Lexie smiled. But she wasn't smiling at Callum. She had just seen the best looking boy on the planet. Who was he? "Who's that?" She asked Saira.

"Dunno. Better ask Holly," Saira said. "Let's get a drink first."

Lexie kept looking over at the boy. They caught up with Holly at last. "Who's that?" Lexie shouted. The music was really loud now.

Holly shook her head. "Don't know. He came with a mate. Nice looking, isn't he? Bit quiet though. Rob says they call him the Rock. Perhaps that's why!"

"Go and say hello," Saira said. "I dare you!"

"Okay!"

Lexie made her way over. "Do you… know this band?" she asked him.

The Rock smiled and shook his head.

"Hey, Lexie!" It was Callum. "Dance with me?" The crowd shifted. Lexie lost sight of the Rock.

A Decision

The next day, Lexie went over to Saira's house after school. Saira was making barfi.

"Mm… that tastes lush!" Lexie said, licking a spoon. "Talking of lush, did you find out any more about that boy at the party?"

"Oh, yes. I spoke to Rob," Saira said. She was adding rosewater to the sweet barfi mixture. It smelt of summer.

"And…"

"And they call him the Rock because he is mad keen on rock climbing," Saira told her.

"Rock climbing?"

"Yes, you know. He is one of the those mad people who climb walls and stuff."

"Isn't there a wall climbing place in that old church by the park?" Lexie asked.

"Yes. He goes there, Rob says."

"Wall climbing..."

"Yes, wall climbing, rock climbing. And forget it. You hate heights."

"I know," Lexie said slowly. It was true. She really was scared of heights. But if that was her only way to get to know the Rock...

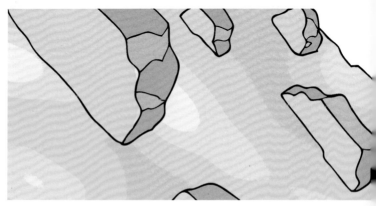

Lexie looked up at the wall. Did anyone climb that thing? It looked too hard.

Had she gone mad?

She hated heights. Her legs felt like jelly. Worse, she could not see the Rock anywhere.

"In your own time," her partner said.
"Remember, move one arm or leg at a
time. Push up with your legs, don't pull
up with your arms."

Lexie put her foot on one of the holds
and pushed herself up. Her leg was
shaking.

"Look for the next handhold, that's it."

Lexie felt for another hold and pushed herself up. The ground was getting further away. She looked around for the Rock. Maybe if he saw her climbing…

"Lexie! Don't lean out like that."

She felt her foot slip. She was going to fall. Her heart was racing. She held on for dear life.

"That's better. Stay close in to the wall."

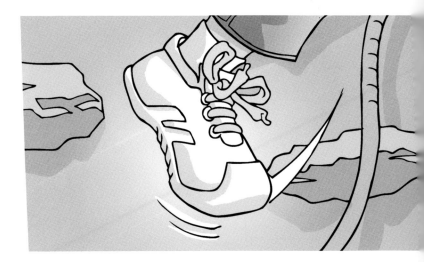

Lexie looked at her feet. Then she saw him. The Rock was there! He smiled up at her.

Okay. He's there. You can do this, Lexie said to herself.

She felt for the footholds.

"That's it, Lexie. Push up with your legs. You're nearly there."

She had reached the top. She was shaking all over.

She looked down. "It's her first time, Jez," her partner said to the Rock.

His name was Jez. He had smiled at her. She couldn't give up now.

Onwards and Upwards

"Lexie, your nails look so bad!"

Saira was painting Lexie's hands with henna. She needed practice for a family wedding.

"Oh, that's from climbing," Lexie said. "You break a nail sometimes. You can't help it."

Saira pulled a face. "And you really like it, this climbing?"

Lexie nodded. "It's great. It gives you a real buzz."

"And Jez? How's that going?"

Lexie looked down at her hands. "That's not going so well," she said.

"He hardly says a word to me."

Saira shook her head. "Face it, Lexie. It's not going to happen," Saira said.

"I need to spend some time with him," Lexie said. "I've had an idea. There's an outdoor rock-climbing course at half term. Jez will be on it. I am going too."

"Outdoor? Isn't that a bit... dangerous," Saira said.

"I know the ropes," Lexie said. "Ropes, get it?"

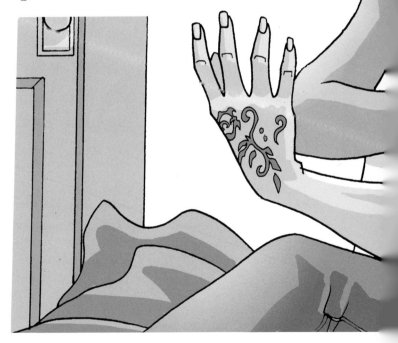

A Challenge

Lexie looked up at the rock. It looked ugly. It had no neat holds, like the climbing wall. Her heart began to thud. Saira was right. This *was* dangerous. What was she doing? She hated heights.

"Okay?" Ruth said. Ruth was Lexie's leader for the climb. "I am going to take it slowly," she told Lexie. "The first pitch will get us there…"

Ruth pointed at a ledge of rock. Lexie gulped. It looked so high.

"You'll be fine!" Ruth said. "Just remember the drill. Keep close to the rock, and make your legs do the work!"

Ruth began climbing. Soon, it was Lexie's turn. Her feet felt for holds. She edged higher. Her eyes searched for the next hold.

It was so different from climbing the wall. The air was crisp. The rock felt warm in the sun. Lexie moved slowly. She was getting higher and higher. At last she reached the ledge.

"Well done, mate!" Ruth said. "That was great for a first climb. Ready for a bit more?"

Lexie looked up. The next bit looked a bit easier. There were gaps and folds in the rock.

"Okay, let's do it!" she said.

That night, the group sat talking for hours at the hostel. Lexie was still on a high from her climb. But Jez wasn't there. Her hopes were going downhill.

Devil's Drop

The week flew by. Lexie felt stronger every day. But she faced her hardest test yet. On the last day, they were climbing Devil's Drop. Lexie had seen pictures at the club. It looked a nightmare. Then she found out she was climbing with Jez. There was no backing out now.

Jez was leader. Lexie watched him climb. He made it look so easy. He reached the first pitch. He gave her the signal. She started to climb. It felt really steep. She couldn't see any footholds. She began to panic. She was leaning out. She knew she mustn't lean too far. It was hard pulling back in. Her arms already hurt.

Don't look down.

Her heart was banging in her chest. She knew she was leaning out too far. She heard a shout. It was Jez. But the wind made it hard to hear.

25

Then she made a mistake.

She looked down.

A toy town valley lay below. It looked so far away.

Lexie panicked. She lost her footing. Her knees banged against the rock face as she fell. Then she felt the rope jerk and lock. She was swinging in space.

Lexie hung there. It seemed like forever. The belay rope creaked. The wind boomed around her.

Don't panic. The rope will hold you. Don't panic.

She felt dizzy. Her mouth was dry. Her hands were wet. They slipped on the rope. What if it snapped? What if she fell?

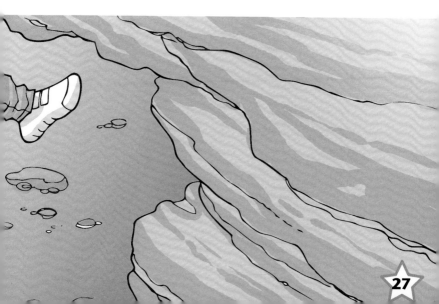

She felt like a dead weight swinging across the rock face.

I can't do this. I can't do this.

She felt giddy and sick.

Then she heard something through the wind.

"You're okay. The rope has got you."

It was Jez.

"Pull yourself in. That's it. The rope has got you. There's a hold right there."

"Jez... I don't think... I can't reach it."

"Yes, you can. It's right there by your foot. That's it."

Lexie felt for the hold.

"Okay. You've got it. You're quite safe.
Push yourself up. That's it."

Somehow she did it. She didn't know how. Jez was so calm. He made her feel safe. She reached the top. She threw her arms round him.
She was shaking all over.

"Thank you!" She said.

"You… you… you were great," Jez smiled.

"I couldn't have done it without you."

"Yes you c… c… could," he blushed. Then it hit Lexie.

So that was it! That was why Jez was always so quiet. He had a stammer.

"S… s… sorry," he said. "I…"

"It's okay, Jez," Lexie said. "I understand. But the way you spoke… back there…"

Jez shrugged.

"I... I had to get you s... s...safe," he said simply.

"It was like we both got over our fears then," Lexie said smiling. She touched his arm.

"I guess so!" Jez said.

"I just thought you didn't want to talk to me!"

Jez shook his head.

"N... no. I..."

"So we have some catching up to do!" Lexie said. That was a bit bold, she thought. But then, she had climbed Devil's Drop!